BELONGS TO: ______________________________

Made in the USA
Monee, IL
04 December 2019

17962002R00069